For The Best Friends We Could Hope For:

Morgan, Bailey, Ryan & Kate

-S.M. & W.B.

Printed in the United States of America by RJ Communications.

ISBN: 978-0-9979074-0-7

Alone in a forest of emerald greens

There napped a small creature, asleep under the trees

He just laid out there dreaming without a care,
He looked just like a rabbit
but
was really a hare.

Out of nowhere there came

loud noises

and

screaming

"There he is!

Now go get him!"

No time left for dreaming.

The chase was on and the hare was quite fast!
But he was still sleepy, he started to gasp...

The men that were after him
had plans for our friend,
They would have him for dinner,
this
would
be
the
end.

The hare turned one last corner
and tripped over some lumber.

He had woken a bear from a deep healthy slumber.

The bear turned around quickly
and let out a tremendous growl.
The hunters ran for their lives,
as the bear sat and scowled.

"Now you can go too!" said the bear to the hare.
He snarled, "leave me alone!"

But the hare was not scared.

"I cannot just leave you," said the hare to the bear.

Since we are now friends!

but the bear, he just stared.

"What is a friend?"

said the bear to the hare.

"I don't think I want one,

I don't think I care!"

Don't be so uptight, So silly, mean and so rude.

Everyone has friends, what's with this attitude?

A friend is there to help you, say if you're in a jam.

A friend will always be there, to lend you a hand.

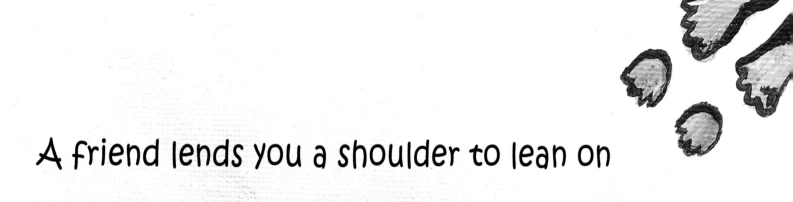

A friend lends you a shoulder to lean on

if he needs to.

If you're happy or sad, a friend will never mislead you.

The bear thought to himself,

if the two of them matched,

He then noticed the hare,

was

starting

to

scratch.

He had a terrible itch on the small of his back,

He could not reach it,

this

was

a

true fact.

He stretched turned and wiggled,

then rolled through some daisies,

He still could not scratch it ,

this was driving him crazy !

The Bear then reached out

with a big hairy paw,

He scratched the hares itch,

with a sharp pointy claw.

The hare was so happy,
he felt oh so good.

He hugged the bear tight, then the bear understood!